TRAVEL THE ANIMAL WORLD

An Atlas of Amazing Creatures

Illustrations by
GIULIA LOMBARDO

Text by
CRISTINA BANFI
RITA MABEL SCHIAVO
CRISTINA PERABONI

WSKids
WHITE STAR KIDS

CONTENTS

This Atlas is not a geography book – it's that and more! Every page is a journey to discovery the world's continents and the animals living there, each in a particular environment where it has found the perfect conditions to live.

You already know many of them, while others may seem strange and mysterious, but there are plenty of incredible, astonishing facts about all of them.

Nature conceals many great surprises that always leave the curious among us amazed and astounded.

You will also meet seven famous people – one for each continent – particularly linked to specific animals, doing everything to protect and save them, at times even paying with their own lives. Their hard work and effort help us understand the importance of protecting our planet's flora and fauna and encourage us to take care of them.

This is why there are also pages dedicated to animals, like the dodo or the quagga, who became extinct in recent centuries. All that remains of them now is hides and bones conserved in museums and old faded photographs. Their end was caused by excessive hunting and the destruction of their environments at the hands of man.

Being aware of their existence and learning about their lives is the first step towards defending other species who are now in danger and attempting to obstruct a fate that we refuse to believe is already marked. Lastly, you will find a fun head-to-head between animals with opposite characteristics that hold true records in nature.

Are you curious to find out who is the fastest and the slowest?

Who is the largest and the smallest?

SO, WHAT ARE YOU WAITING FOR? START READING...

THE BIOMES

PACIFIC OCEAN
ATLANTIC OCEAN
ANTARCTIC OCEAN
Polar desert
Tundra
Taiga
Grasslands
Temperate forest
Rainforest
Savannah/Tropical grasslands/ Mediterranean scrub
Hot desert

It is the wide variety of environments that makes our planet special. From the poles to the equator, the climate changes radically, mainly characterized by temperature and humidity. Also depending on the conformation of the land and the presence of rivers or mountain ranges, the biomes range from cold, desolate ice to lush, tropical forests.

RAINFOREST, TEMPERATE FOREST, TAIGA

What is a forest? Easy, it's a place that has a large number of trees.

But not all forests are the same. Moving away from the equator towards the poles, the climate changes and we find gradually different species of trees.

Tropical forests, or rainforests, where it rains almost every day, are the planet's most luxuriant forests. In the warm, humid climate of the tropics, the trees are always green and grow close to each other, reaching great heights in an ongoing battle for more light.

The forests of temperate climates, like ours, are characterized by broad-leaved trees with large, jagged-edged leaves that shed in fall and grow again in spring. The undergrowth in a temperate forest, made up of shorter bushes and plants, is often as rich and impenetrable as a tropical forest.

Moving towards the poles, the climate gets increasingly colder. The forests above all feature conifers, like fir trees and other plants with needle-type leaves. This forest is called "taiga".

HOT DESERTS, POLAR DESERTS, ICE SHEETS

The word "desert" means "abandoned" and suggests a place where there is no life. Indeed, desert areas are so inhospitable that only a few species of very well adapted plants and animals manage to live there. The reason is that it rarely or almost never rains in the desert and, as you well know, water is a vital element for survival.

There are two types of desert in the world and each desert has different characteristics: they range from the boundless expanses of sandy dunes in northern Africa's Sahara, the largest hot desert on our planet, to the cold Gobi Desert in central Asia, where temperatures can fall well below freezing in winter.

And, finally, it might seem strange, but the world's largest desert is Antarctica: it is a genuine desert of ice!

GRASSLANDS, SAVANNAH, STEPPES, TUNDRA

There is a family of plants which are, so to speak, "born to be eaten." These are grasses, which can be grazed by animals without depleting as they continue to grow and sprout leaves little by little as they are cut back. The world's great grasslands exist thanks to these plants.

These are immense seas of grass, where numerous packs of animals pasture: antelopes, zebras, and buffalo in the Africa savannah, or herds of bison in the great plains of North America.

Meanwhile, a steppe is the typical grassland of central Asia, where grasses grow alongside low woody plants. This is the perfect environment for wild horses.

Moving northwards, we come to the tundra, stretches of moss, lichen, and small shrubs that resist the cold and grow on land where the subsoil is perpetually frozen.

COASTS, CORAL REEFS, OPEN SEA, ABYSSES

The seas cover two-thirds of the planet's surface and host a large variety of environments, from the shores of the continents to the deepest abysses.

Coastal landscapes may feature sandy beaches or rocky cliffs, or even saltwater lagoons, where plants and animals have adapted to living both in and out of the water, whose level rises and falls with the turning of the tides.

In the warm waters of the tropics, the corals are stretches of reef – indeed they are called coral reefs – populated by an infinite variety of fish and other vividly-colored animals.

The open sea is the vastest environment and is home to the largest mass of living organisms in the world. This is why gigantic whales find enough food to feed on.

Light gradually dims as you descend from the surface towards the marine depths. Bizarrely-shaped fish and strange abyssal animals live at depths of even thousands of feet, where darkness reigns and the pressure is so strong that it could crush a submarine.

EUROPE

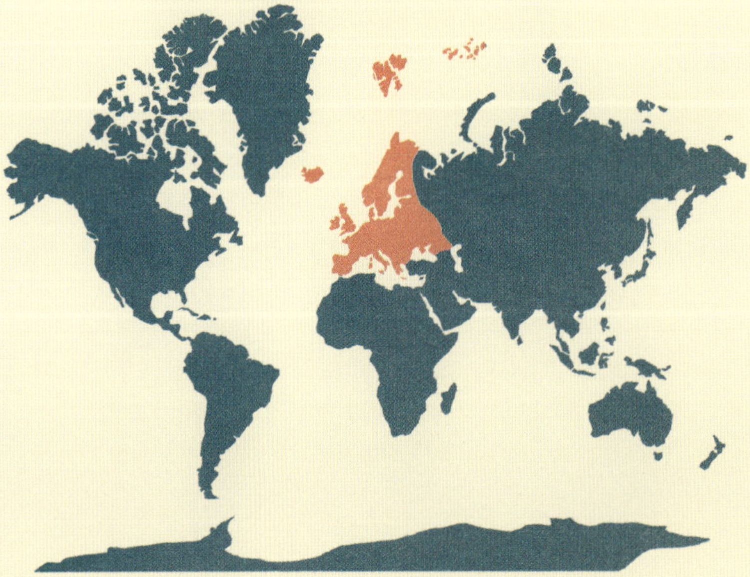

The continent of Europe has a smaller surface area than Oceania, but it has the third highest population. This is due to the lack of inhospitable areas, such as deserts or ice sheets, and also its prevalently temperate climate.

Its borders are mainly marked by seas: the Arctic Ocean to the north, the Atlantic Ocean to the west, and the Mediterranean Sea and the Black Sea to the south. To the east lies Asia, whose border is not well established as it is based on historical, political, and economic facts rather than physical elements. It is often considered to be the border of the Ural mountain range.

The variety of vegetation and fauna is most of all due to altitude, given the great abundance of coasts and high mountain ranges.

LEMMING

Its round body, short limbs, and tiny ears limit heat loss for this little rodent that lives in the Arctic tundra. It does not hibernate and, during the years of mass reproduction, the young are forced to embark on long migrations. When they get to the coast, they dive in as able swimmers and try to reach new lands but die in the thousands in the strong waves of the cold seas.

VIVIPAROUS LIZARD

This lizard can live farther north and at higher latitudes in mountains than any other. This is why it keeps its eggs warm in its body until they hatch. It gives birth to little babies already formed and wrapped in a semi-transparent membrane. Actually, it is an ovoviviparous reptile.

GOLDEN EAGLE

Up to 35 inches (90 cm) in length, it is adapted to hunting in open environments at high altitudes. It hunts hares and other birds by seizing them with its claws after a sidelong dive. The female golden eagle lays two eggs in a large nest of branches built on a cliff, but usually only one of the two baby eagles manages to fly off around the middle of May.

DEER

Deer are large herbivores that can weigh over 700 pounds (300 kg). During the mating season, the bucks have long branched horns, called antlers. Made of bone, they weigh up to 30 pounds (15 kg) and they are shed and grow back every year. The call of the deer is called a bellow.

ROE DEER

The roe deer is the smallest species of deer and its smaller antlers have very few points. Its tail is short so that it doesn't cover the white rump patch that is larger in dominating bucks and helps keep the herd together.

IBEX

Adapted to the rocky terrain of the high mountains, its hooves are like suction cups so that it won't slip. The males have large horns shaped like sabers. They feature dark horizontal lines, rings of growth that we can use to tell the goat's age.

WOLF

Ancestors of domestic dogs, wolves are strong carnivores that live in packs. Within the pack, fights determine the alpha male and female, though no wounds are caused. These are the leaders that all the others must submit to and they are the only ones who can reproduce.

WILDCAT

Similar to domestic cats, they have yellowish-green eyes with vertical pupils. They have very bushy ringed tails cut off at the tip. Solitary and crepuscular and nocturnal in their habits, wildcats catch small prey, especially rodents and birds. They leave many scented traces to mark their territory.

RED FOX

Thanks to their great adaption skills, foxes have managed to survive despite intense hunting. They have an excellent sense of smell and superb hearing – they can hear a mouse squeaking at 330 feet (100 m). Their soft red fur is even thicker in their tails, so they use them as a "blanket" during the cold period.

LYNX

The lynx is the largest European feline. It hunts by stalking and jumping on its prey and can even catch a young deer. Generally solitary, it ranges over large areas, marking its territory. Its eyesight is famous, but its hearing is just as good. It has characteristic tufts of black fur on its ears.

BADGER

Crepuscular and nocturnal, badgers are omnivores with typical black and white coloring on their heads. They dig vast underground dens with their strong claws, where long tunnels unite numerous chambers. Multiple families can live in some "setts".

POLECAT

They use their anal scent glands to mark their territory like all mustelids, but, like skunks, their secretion is particularly stinky and can be sprayed for defense. The polecat's typical feature is the mask-like pattern on its face. The ferret is the domestic descendent of the polecat.

OTTER

These carnivores mainly feed on fish and are able swimmers. They are well adapted to life in the water thanks to their streamlined form, small ears, webbed paws, flat tail that they can use as a rudder, and waterproof fur. This is a threatened species, especially due to pollution of the waterways.

MOLE

These are insectivores that are capable of eating more than their own weight in food every day. They spend most of their time in the underground tunnels that they dig with their long back legs equipped with as many as six claws! Their extra thumb is the extension of a wrist bone.

WHITE STORK

They come to Europe in springtime and each pair returns to the nest they had built in a roof or bell-tower. This is why they are a symbol of rebirth. They feed on fish and amphibians in the low waters of ponds and paddy fields, walking through them on their long legs.

BUSTARD

They can be considered the heaviest flying bird, even though they prefer to walk in the open environs of grasslands. In springtime, the males perform showy parades to win over the females. The latter then nest and raise the young by themselves.

LONG-EARED BAT

These bats, which are 1.5-2 inches (4-5 cm) in length, are easy to recognize due to their huge ears. When at rest, they flatten out their ears behind them and hide them under their wings. They feed on moths, beetles, and mosquitos that they catch in the brush, parks, or gardens where they live.

PEREGRINE FALCON

They have a dark head, similar to the hood worn by pilgrims, and they are considered the fastest animal. They can dive at over 180 miles (300 km) per hour! Like other falcons, the female is larger than the male. It is the most widely used species in falconry.

COMMON KINGFISHER

This is one of Europe's most colorful birds, with its reddish breast and bright blue back. Its nest is made up of a chamber at the end of a tunnel dug into the embankment of rivers, lakes, or ponds. In order to catch the little fish that it feeds on, it dives into the water after first spotting them from a perch.

MONK SEAL

Typical of the Mediterranean Sea, this seal is under serious threat of extinction. Hunted by fishermen because it feeds on fish, it is sensitive to the disturbance caused by tourism and takes refuge in sea caves. It gives birth to a pup every 2 or 3 years. Relaxed and sedentary, it lives in small colonies and can climb rocks thanks to the digits of its rear fin.

LOGGERHEAD SEA TURTLE

Like all sea turtles, its legs have evolved into fins and it has a flat carapace to make it hydrodynamic. It lives in temperate waters and feeds on mollusks, crustaceans, fish, echinoderms, and jellyfish. A female can lay up to 200 eggs in holes dug into the sand at beaches. This species is at risk of extinction.

SWORDFISH

This speedy, agile swimmer can measure over 15 feet (4.5 m) in length and weigh over 880 pounds (400 kg). It is famous for its upper jawbone that forms a sword that is one-third the length of its body. It preys on fish, crustaceans, and squid by striking them with its sword (not by piercing them!).

FIN WHALE

Thanks to its tapering shape and flat head, this is the fastest whale. It can reach speeds of up to 20 miles (33 km) per hour. When it filters water through its baleen, its throat grooves expand, enabling it to swallow fish, as well as krill. This giant of the sea can live for up to 80 years and reach up to 80 feet (25 m) in length and 75 tons in weight.

SPERM WHALE

These are easily recognized due to their huge, rectangular heads, which contain an oily substance that changes density depending on temperature and depth, helping the whale in its hydrostatic drive. This means it can descend into the abysses in the search for its favorite prey: the giant squid. It is considered the world's largest carnivore.

JACKAL

Typically reddish in color, the jackal is much smaller than a wolf, but in packs it can even attack sheep or goats. They form stable couples that live together all their lives and both parents look after the young.

KONRAD LORENZ AND GRAYLAG GEESE

He is considered the father of ethology, i.e., the study of animal behavior. Together with Tinbergen and Von Frisch, he won the Nobel Prize for his studies. He was born in Vienna in 1903 and graduated in both medicine and zoology. His passion was animals, which he mainly wanted to observe freely living in nature.

He became famous to the wider public for his book "King Solomon's Ring," where he describes his scientific studies in an educational way. In the introduction, he explains that neither scientific method nor great patience is enough for studying animals if there is no complicity and love.

Lorenz analyzed the behavior of graylag geese in depth. The most famous of these was Martina. Lorenz was the first living thing that Martina saw after hatching and so she saw him as her "mother". She would follow him everywhere, learning everything he taught her. This premature learning was defined "imprinting".

Graylag geese live in groups and mainly feed on water plants. The male and female build the nest together on land and look after the young. They are migratory animals who form classic V-shape flight formations.

AFRICA

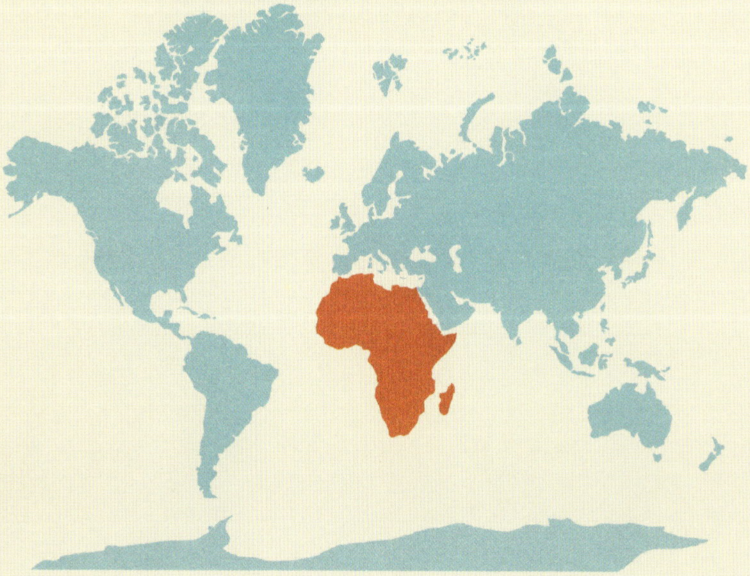

Africa is the second largest continent after Asia. Its coasts are washed by the Mediterranean Sea, the Red Sea, the Indian Ocean, and the Atlantic Ocean.

It has a large area in both the northern and southern hemispheres, hence its various types of environments where a large variety of animals live. In particular, the savannah is home to the largest land animals currently living.

Just off the African coast, there are many archipelagos and a large island, Madagascar, with its unique fauna and flora.

Equator

DROMEDARY

Also known as the "ship of the desert", the dromedary has unrivalled physical resistance and can go without drinking for an entire week. The people living in the Sahara Desert have been using it as a pack animal and to move from one oasis to the next for the past two thousand years.

FENNEC

Weighing just 3.3 pounds (1.5 kg), the fennec, or desert fox, is the smallest fox in the world. Its large ears obviously give it great hearing, but also help disperse heat more quickly, vital considering the torrid environment it lives in.

LAPPET-FACED VULTURE

The lappet-faced vulture, or Nubian vulture, is the most powerful African vulture and it prevails over all other animals that ravenously mill around a carcass. Not only does it eat carrion, it also actively hunts small prey or raids the nests of other birds.

LESSER FLAMINGO

The lesser flamingo is an elegant bird with bright pink plumage. It forms stable pairs and lives in extremely large colonies of even a million individual birds. A colony of these flamingos taking flight is one of Africa's most extraordinary sights.

MARABOU STORK

The marabou is a relation of our storks, but its lifestyle is more like that of a vulture. It is an animal of impressive size, 60 inches (150 cm) high and with a wingspan of 10 feet (3 m). Its large beak means it can easily shred the carrion it feeds on.

The Nile crocodile is the largest African crocodile, reaching up to 20 feet (6 m) in length. It lives in the freshwaters all over the African continent, from Egypt to South Africa. Its bite is extremely strong and can grind up any animal within reach, even a large buffalo.

NILE CROCODILE

ZEBRA

The zebra is a large herbivore of the savannah. Its black and white striped coat helps the animal hide among the light and shadow of the large grasses. Every pattern is unique to each animal, like a fingerprint. Indeed, there are no two zebras exactly alike.

AARDVARK

The aardvark is also called the African anteater. It feeds exclusively on termites, catching large numbers of them with its long sticky tongue after demolishing their nest using its large claws. It digs its den in the ground and spends the daylight hours there, only coming out at night.

GNU

This is one of the most common herbivores in the savannah. Gnus embark on an epic migration every year: 1.6 million individuals move en masse in search of pasturage and water, from Tanzania to Kenya, completing a journey of over 500 miles (800 km). In every migration, 250,000 gnus are killed by predators or die of exhaustion from the journey.

OSTRICH

The ostrich holds many records among birds. It is the largest, reaching over 8.2 feet (2.5 m) in height and weighing up to 330 pounds (150 kg). It is the fastest at running, exceeding 50 miles (80 km) per hour. And it lays the largest eggs, 6 inches (15 cm) long, the equivalent of around 20 hen's eggs.

MONGOOSE

The mongoose is a small mammal that has a great skill: its guile, courage, and lightning-fast reflexes make it a snake's most ferocious enemy. The mongoose is one of few animals able to confront a cobra, as it can avoid its mortal attacks and kill it by biting its neck.

WARTHOG

Despite its less than reassuring appearance, the warthog is not a particularly aggressive animal. However, if threatened, it can defend itself very well by biting. It loves rolling around in mud and it curiously holds its tail up high, like an antenna, when running.

ELEPHANT

With its height of almost 13 feet (4 m) and almost weighing the equivalent of five cars, we can call the elephant the true king of the savannah. This pachyderm lives in a matriarchal society; each herd is led by the oldest female.

GIRAFFE

The giraffe is the world's tallest animal. The male can reach up to 20 feet (6 m) in height. It feeds on the leaves of acacia, which it tears from the branches with a swipe of its long, extremely coarse tongue, oblivious to the thorns.

LION

Lions live in the savannah in prides. They spend the day alternating long hours of sleep in the shade of the few trees around with short hunts, most often carried out by the females. Their prey are gazelle, antelopes, and also large animals, such as giraffes and buffalo.

IMPALA

The impala is an elegant and extremely agile antelope that can bounce up to 30 feet (10 m). The males have horns in the shape of a lyre and perform ritual duels. They face each other with their heads down, making grunting sounds.

LEOPARD

The leopard is perhaps the world's most beautiful and elegant predator. It always moves slowly, silently, and watchfully, but when it springs, it is extremely fast and can catch an antelope of 110 pounds (50 kg) and, once killed, carry it up onto a tree branch to eat its meal in complete peace.

BUFFALO

The African buffalo is always found in the savannah. In a grazing herd, there is always a vigilant male with its head held high and curved horns in plain view. Its black silhouette is unmistakable, even from far away, and elicits fear and respect.

BABOON

Baboons are a type of monkey that prefer to stay on the ground rather than in the trees. They live in large groups under the protection of very strong males equipped with sharp canine teeth. They mainly feed on vegetation but occasionally also eat small animals.

RHINOCEROS

The black rhinoceros is distinguished from the white rhinoceros not by its color, but rather by its upper lip, which is pointed rather than flat. This species is under great threat from poachers who hunt it for its horn, which is sold on the black market at high prices.

CHAMELEON

This reptile is known for its ability to camouflage itself by changing the color of its skin. However, it has other characteristics too. Its eyes rotate independently from each other; its tail is prehensile; and its tongue can extend to twice its body length, very useful for catching the insects it feeds on.

LEMUR

These prosimians are almost all nocturnal and their calls can be heard among the trees of the forest, similar to the shouts of children at play. There are different species of lemur, who all live in Madagascar, except for one who is native to the nearby Comoros.

AFRICAN PENGUIN

The African penguins live along the western coasts of South Africa and Namibia. They gave their name to the Penguin Islands where great numbers of them live. They live in large colonies, though they have suffered great losses in recent decades due to the oil pollution of the sea.

WHITE SHARK

With triangular teeth of up to 3 inches (7.5 cm) in length, the white shark is the largest predator fish. It can exceed 20 feet (6 m) in length and 440 pounds (200 kg) in weight. It is found in oceans all over the world and also lives in the Mediterranean Sea. White sharks are plentiful along the coast of South Africa, where their preferred prey are sea lions.

DIAN FOSSEY AND THE GORILLAS

Dian Fossey was an American naturalist who loved animals. She dedicated 20 years of her life to studying gorillas and founded a research center in the equatorial forest of Rwanda to protect them.

She would spend many hours a day in their company, observing their behavior and even becoming accepted as a member of their group.

Her diligent work against poachers who were drastically reducing the number of gorillas led to her death. Indeed, she was murdered by an unknown person in 1985.

Gorillas are the largest monkeys on the planet. Even though they may seem threatening, they are actually shy and non-aggressive animals. They live in family groups protected by an elderly male distinguished by the silver-grey fur on its back, thus called a silverback.

Gorillas are very intelligent and communicate with each other through their body posture and also by making different sounds. They feed on large quantities of vegetation, fruit, and leaves, and are able to build a nest for the nighttime on land or high up in trees.

ASIA

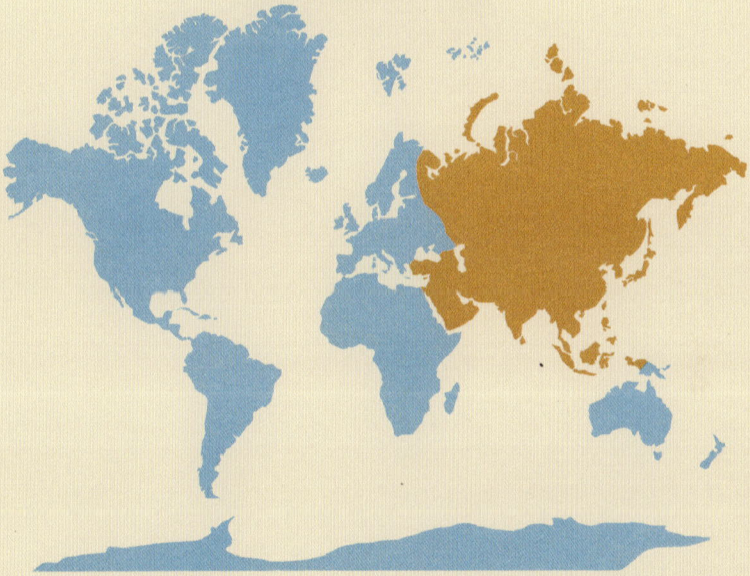

Measuring four times the surface area of Europe, Asia is the largest continent. It is washed by the Pacific, Indian, and Arctic Oceans, as well as the Mediterranean Sea. It is joined to Europe to form Eurasia, while it connects to Africa at the Isthmus of Suez and to North America at the Bering Strait.

Asia is also the continent of great contrasts: here we find Everest, 29,029 feet (8848 m), the world's highest mountain, and the Mariana Trench, -36,070 feet (10,994 m), the deepest point on Earth. Temperatures range from -158 °F (-70 °C) in the Siberian tundra to 129 °F (54 °C) in the Iranian desert, passing through all types of environments, from taiga, steppe, and savannah to tropical forest. Therefore, both fauna and flora are very diverse. Asia is home to northern lichen and reindeer, but also palm trees, fruit trees, and camels.

NARWHAL

The narwhal is a cetacean that lives in the freezing arctic seas, and it is the mammal with the most northern area of distribution. Of the two teeth they possess, the upper left tooth of the male grows up to 8 feet (2.5 m) in a helix spiral that protrudes from the mouth through its lip. The function of this long tooth is still uncertain and is debated by zoologists.

ARCTIC FOX

Its short legs with hairy paw pads, small ears, short head, and warm coat allow this fox to survive the long freezing winters of the Arctic. In winter its fur is generally white, whereas in summer it becomes light brown.
In some populations along the coast, its winter coat is blueish-silver.

YAK

Domesticated by man for its wool, meat, milk, and as a means of transport, it is now rare to find it in the wild. The yak only lives in herds in the frozen steppes. Its black fur manages to protect it from intense cold at up to 19,685 feet (6000 m) above sea level, where it uses ice as a source of water.

SNOW LEOPARD

This is a leopard with thick, woolly fur that is light grey or creamy in color, featuring large dark rosettes that make it spotted. Its great agility allows it to move around the rocks of the mountains where it lives. The snow leopard can meow, yelp, or purr, but it cannot roar.

TIGER

Its streaked coat enables the tiger to camouflage itself among the shadows of the forest. It lives a solitary life and loves terrains that are rich in water. Once it spots its prey, it pounces on it and kills it by a blow to the neck with its paw. The Siberian tiger can reach up to 660 pounds (300 kg) and is the largest modern-day feline.

CAMEL

The wild camels live in the cold Gobi Desert, where they can stand temperatures of up to -68 °F (-20 °C). They can walk on snow without sinking thanks to their wide hooves. Their two humps are reserves of fat and stand up straight when the animal is well nourished, otherwise they fall to the side.

RED PANDA

Even though its name might fool you, this is not a bear, but rather a close relation of the American raccoon. Like giant pandas, it mainly feeds on bamboo and vegetation and it has a false thumb for grabbing shoots. It lives in the mountains of Nepal and China.

KOI FISH

The koi fish is considered a symbol of wealth, love, and luck in Japan. Various species were selected by breeders in ancient China to make an ornamental fish. Today it is found in many private ponds, fountains, and lakes all over the world. The koi fish is also the longest living fish, reaching a record age of 226 years.

ASIAN ELEPHANT

Compared to the African elephant, the Asian variety is smaller, with more minute, round ears, and with just one prehensile lip at the end of its trunk. Absent in females, even their tusks are shorter. These elephants also live in matriarchal groups headed by an elderly female who leads the group in the search for water and food.

ASIAN LION

This is a subspecies of lion, now relegated to the Gir National Park in India. It is a bit smaller than its African relation and its mane is not as thick, but its habits are similar. In recent years, various conservation projects have succeeded in bringing its numbers up slightly.

INDIAN RHINOCEROS

It has one horn and it is a very imposing animal, reaching up to 2 tons in weight. Its hide does not have any fur and features numerous folds and tubercles on its flanks and rear, giving an overall impression of a suit of armor. Among the folds hide many parasites who are removed by various birds, thus keeping the rhino's skin clean.

BABIRUSA

It belongs to the family of pigs. Its skin is greyish-brown and wrinkled, with a few hairs here and there. The male has two upper canines that constantly grow and can exceed 12 inches (30 cm) in length! They grow upwards, piercing first the upper lip and then the palate, and stick up on their heads like horns.

PANGOLIN

Its body is covered in thick scales that can be tilted at will and are periodically replaced. These guarantee the pangolin protection from predators and camouflage in the environment. It has strong back legs with thick claws for digging. Its prehensile tail makes it a tree-climbing animal. It is a glutton for ants and termites, which it catches with its long tongue.

PEAFOWL

This bird is native to the tropical forests of India. The males have brightly-colored feathers, while the females have camouflage plumage that hides them while they are brooding eggs in nests built on the ground. To attract the female during the courtship rituals, the male displays a multi-colored wheel with its tail feathers that can reach up to 80 inches (2 m).

RED-CROWNED CRANE

Bolstered by its 55-inch (140 cm) height, this crane moves through the marshy grasslands, dominating the environment from above. It feeds on small water animals that it catches using its long sharp beak. During the mating season, couples engage in spectacular dances. They remain faithful to each other their entire lives.

DALMATIAN PELICAN

This is a large bird with white plumage and black tips on its feathers. It is unique and recognizable due to the pink or orange pouch under its beak, which the animal uses to catch the fish it feeds on. It often lives and hunts in groups. Various individuals cooperate to drive a shoal of fish to low waters for easier hunting.

INDIAN COBRA

Feared for its powerful mortal venom, this snake is generally a timid, mild-mannered animal, but if it feels threatened it immediately raises its head and upper body. By stretching the skin of its neck, it displays marks that look like a pair of eyes. It also emits a hiss as a warning sign.

GIBBON

This is a small monkey that lives in the rainforests of southeast Asia, where it moves around by nimbly swinging from tree to tree with the strength of its long arms and never goes down to ground level. Like gorillas and chimpanzees, gibbons have no tail. However, some have throat sacs that amplify their voices.

LONG-NOSED MONKEY

This tree-living monkey lives along the rivers and in the mangrove forests of Borneo. Its name comes from its unusual long hanging nose that is more evident in males than in females. The long-nosed monkey lives in groups of up to 30 individuals comprising a dominant male and females with their young. The male sees to protecting the group, while the females look after gathering food.

SUGAR GLIDER

This is a small nocturnal tree-living marsupial that we find in New Guinea and Indonesia. Thanks to the membrane joining its legs together, it can launch itself from a few feet up into long jumping glides, covering distances of up to 165 feet (50 m). It prefers sweet-tasting food, such as fruit, but does not turn its nose up at insects when necessary.

BIRD-OF-PARADISE

This group contains many different species of varying sizes. The males are fitted out with gaudily-colored plumage and unusual decorations which are flaunted at their courting rituals to win over the females. The "dances" are performed on tree branches and can last many hours. These forest birds feed on fruit.

KOMODO DRAGON

This is a very large lizard that can reach up to 10 feet (3 m) in length and 150 pounds (70 kg) in weight. As an adult, it feeds mostly on deer, which it pounces on and bites. Its bite infects the wound with poison that allows no escape. The komodo dragon can swallow a meal of up to 80% of its bodyweight in one go.

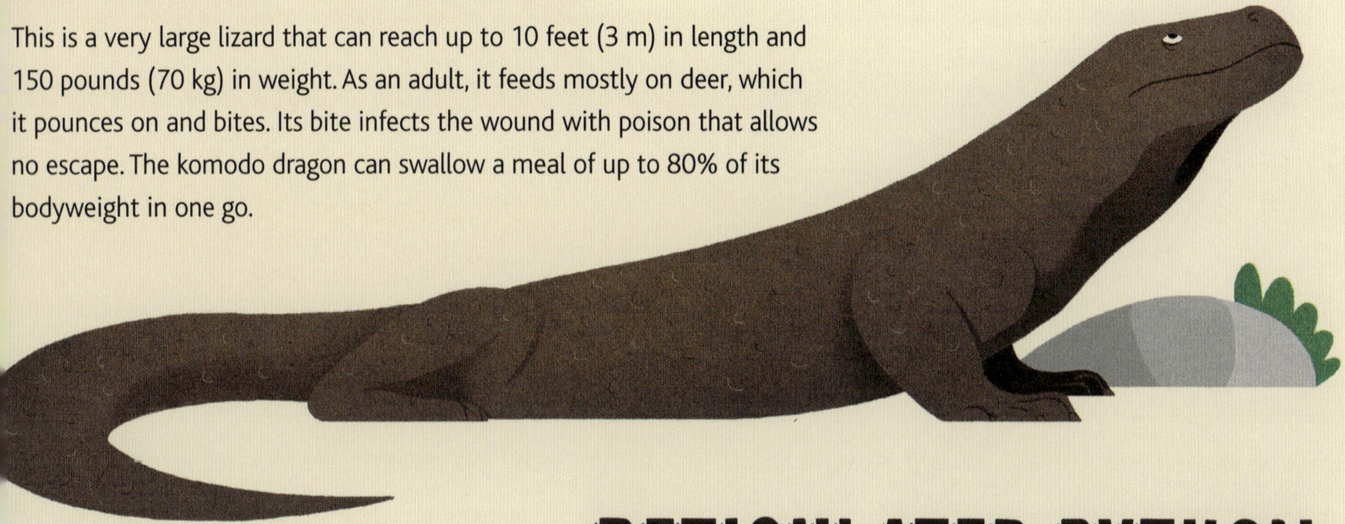

RETICULATED PYTHON

The quite slender body of this snake can easily reach up to 30 feet (9 m) in length and 300 pounds (140 kg) in weight. It lives in forests and humid areas, including canals in inhabited areas, where it feeds on the often-abundant numbers of rats that it finds thanks to the special clefts in its lips that can detect the presence of hot-blooded prey.

FLYING DRAGON

This small lizard of roughly 8 inches (20 cm) lives among the trees of the tropical forests where it hunts insects. The flying dragons can jump from trees and glide for over 50 feet (15 m). For this type of flight, they do not have actual wings, but flaps of skin on their sides. The animal unfolds them when needed to form a kind of sail.

ARMAND DAVID AND THE GIANT PANDA

The young Armand David joined a congregation of missionaries so that he could continue his studies, which would otherwise have been too expensive for his family. As he was passionate about plants and animals and had great naturalistic knowledge, he was sent to evangelize the populations of Asia in the mid-19th century, at the same time gathering evidence, first of all in China, and subsequently also in Mongolia and Tibet.

During his scientific wanderings, he described various species for the first time, such as summer lilac, which is now found in our gardens as it attracts butterflies, along with the milu deer and, above all, the giant panda.

The symbol of WWF, the giant panda is considered one of the top 100 species at most risk of extinction. The panda is a vegetarian bear with characteristic black and white thick fur and a peaceful temperament. During the day, it spends at least 12 hours sitting comfortably eating more than 25 pounds (12 kg) of bamboo shoots, the plant it mainly feeds on. For gathering shoots, it has a "false thumb" deriving from the lengthening of a wrist bone, making its paw look like it has six fingers!

Today the giant panda only lives in the wild in the mountainous areas of central China. However, it is reared in captivity in some zoological gardens. The young that are born are owned by the Chinese government, which uses them to create a genetic bank to guarantee the panda's future.

OCEANIA

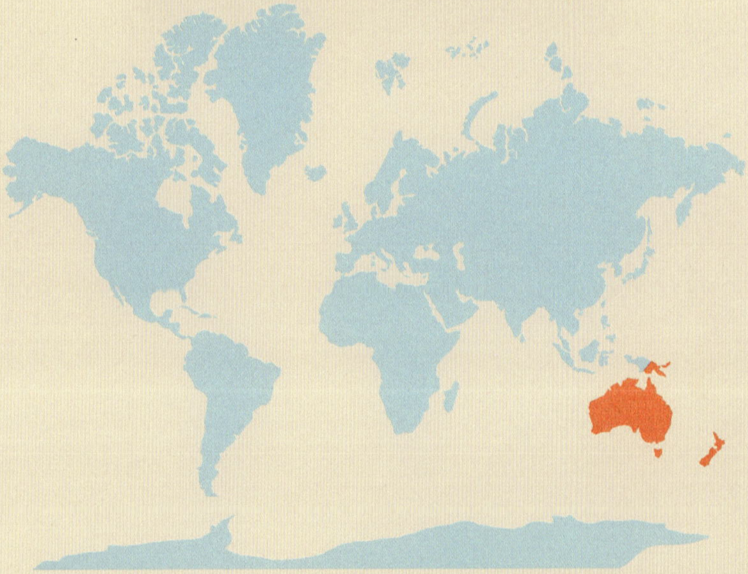

Oceania comprises Australia, New Zealand, Polynesia, Melanesia, and Micronesia.

The total surface area, including all of the islands, covers over 3 million square miles (9 million square kilometers), with Australia making up almost 90% by itself.

The islands of Micronesia and Polynesia are located along the equator in vast ocean spaces – justifying the name of the continent – and have a tropical climate. The southern part of Australia and New Zealand, on the other hand, are located much more to the south and have a climate that gets gradually colder.

DUGONG

A relation of the American and African manatees, the dugong is a large aquatic mammal that is roughly 10 feet (3 m) in length and reaches up to half a ton in weight. It lives in the lower waters along the coasts of the Indo-Pacific, where it solely grazes on water plants.

SALTWATER CROCODILE

The saltwater crocodile is the world's largest crocodile. It can reach up to 20 feet (6 m) in length and a ton in weight. It lives in coastal swamps, but lays its eggs in nests built near freshwater, where they are "lovingly" taken care of until they hatch.

WHALE SHARK

The whale shark gets its name from its size, which competes with that of cetaceans like the whale. Indeed, with a length of over 50 feet (15 m), it is the largest shark in the world. In addition, like the whale, it only feeds on plankton, shrimp, small fish, and small squid.

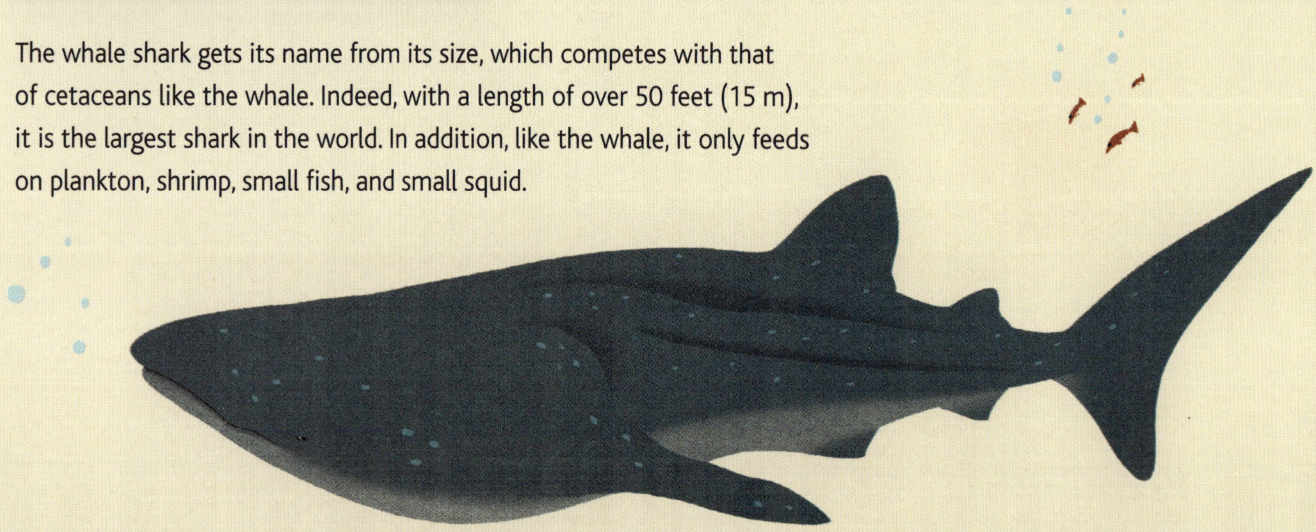

WOMBAT

The wombat is a marsupial that looks like a little bear. It grows up to 3 feet (1 m) in length and weighs around 65 pounds (30 kg). Its dens are made up of a series of very long tunnels, where it can quickly take refuge if a predator arrives.

STONEFISH

It can be dangerous to rummage around the underwater rocks of a coral reef, because you could touch a stonefish, which looks just like a stone encrusted with algae and coral. Its spikes can inject you with a strong poison which is often deadly.

ECHIDNA

The echidna is a bizarre mammal that looks like a cocktail of many different animals. It is covered with spikes like a hedgehog, has the long face of an anteater and the claws of a bear, and lays eggs like a bird!

PLATYPUS

It is also known as the duck-billed platypus and it is easy to see why! It lays eggs, like the echidna, and it is the only mammal that has its own poison, located in the spurs of its hind legs. A skillful swimmer, it is much more at home in water than on land.

MOLOCH

Given its alarming appearance, the moloch could compete with the most terrifying dinosaurs if it weren't just 8 inches (20 cm) long. It is fully mimetic; in fact, its body bristling with spikes and tubercles makes it look like a dry thorny branch.

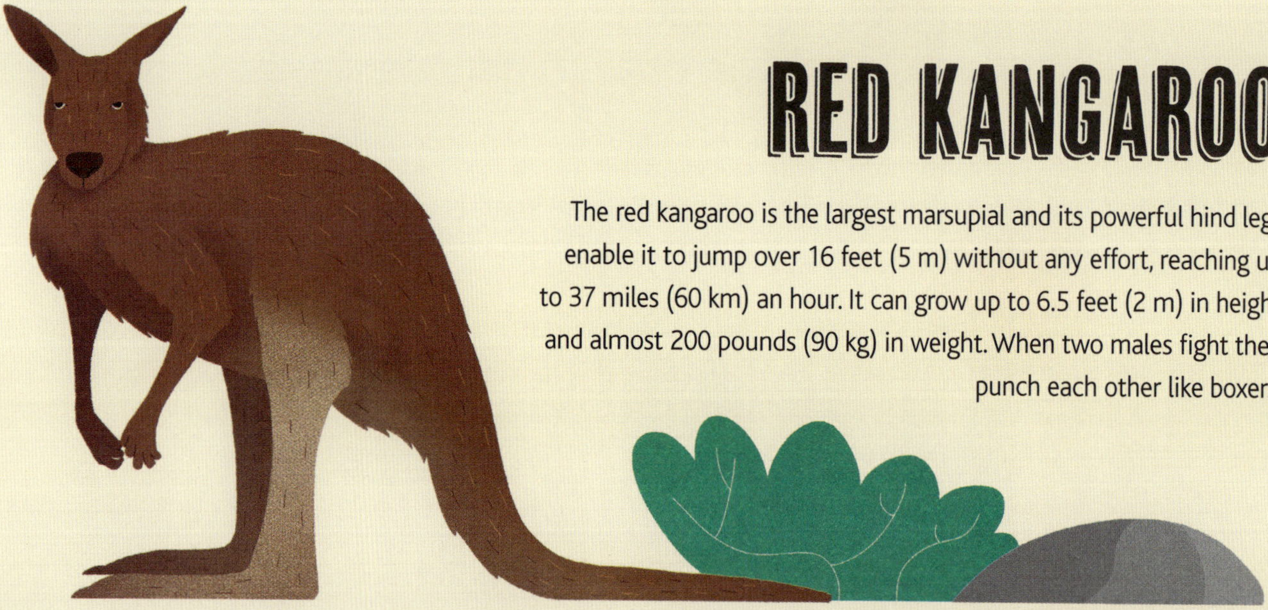

RED KANGAROO

The red kangaroo is the largest marsupial and its powerful hind legs enable it to jump over 16 feet (5 m) without any effort, reaching up to 37 miles (60 km) an hour. It can grow up to 6.5 feet (2 m) in height and almost 200 pounds (90 kg) in weight. When two males fight they punch each other like boxers.

KOALA

The koala is a docile animal that spends its life among the branches of eucalyptus trees whose leaves are its only food. It looks cuddly like a little bear, but it is a marsupial. When the young have developed, they climb onto the mother's back and are carried around until they become self-sufficient.

WALLABY

Many smaller species of kangaroo are called wallabies, which derives from the aboriginal name. More graceful than the large kangaroos, the wallabies have been introduced into many places far from their native land.

QUOKKA

The quokka is a small marsupial native to south-western Australia. Looking like a toy kangaroo, it is approximately 20 inches (50 cm) long and weighs less than 11 pounds (5 kg). Despite its awkward appearance, it is very agile and is sociable when approached.

COCKATOO

A typical Australian parrot, the cockatoo is unmistakable when it raises the crest of feathers it has on its head. Its size and color vary from the small pink cockatoo, as big as a pigeon, to the impressive black cockatoo, 24 inches (60 cm) in length, which has the largest beak among the parrot family.

EMU

Also known as the Australian ostrich, the emu is a fast runner like its African relation. It has soft plumage which ripples in the wind when it runs and areas of naked skin that are blue on the head and neck.

KOOKABURRA

The kookaburra is similar to Europe's common kingfisher, but it is much larger and feeds on mice, lizards, and insects. Its strange name comes from the aboriginal name and refers to its call, which is identical to a laughing sound.

CASSOWARY

The cassowary is a large flightless bird. Its wings have evolved into a series of long quills, black like the rest of its plumage. The bright red and blue colors of its neck and head are a sign of danger. The cassowary is well able to defend itself with its long, sharp claws.

LYREBIRD

Normally the mimetic color of the lyrebird means it is not very eye-catching, but during courting, the male displays all its beauty by opening its tail feathers and rippling them like a delicate bridal veil.

TUATARA

At first sight, the tuatara looks simply like a large lizard, but experts consider it a "living fossil" as it is the only surviving species of a group of reptiles that became extinct 60 million years ago. It lives on the islands of New Zealand and is now a protected species.

KIWI

The kiwi's strange appearance would be enough in itself to make it different than all other birds, but it also has a more hidden unique characteristic: the female, which is as big as a hen, lays eggs that weigh almost a pound (0.5 kg)!

ABEL TASMAN

Abel Tasman was a Dutch navigator and explorer in the 17th century. He was the first to reach the islands of Tasmania, which were named after him, and New Zealand. He is also credited with drawing up the geographical maps of regions still unexplored at that time. Tasman did not receive great recognition from the Dutch East India Company that financed his expeditions, because the lands he discovered had more scientific than economic value. In fact, Tasmania and New Zealand were not visited again for over a century.

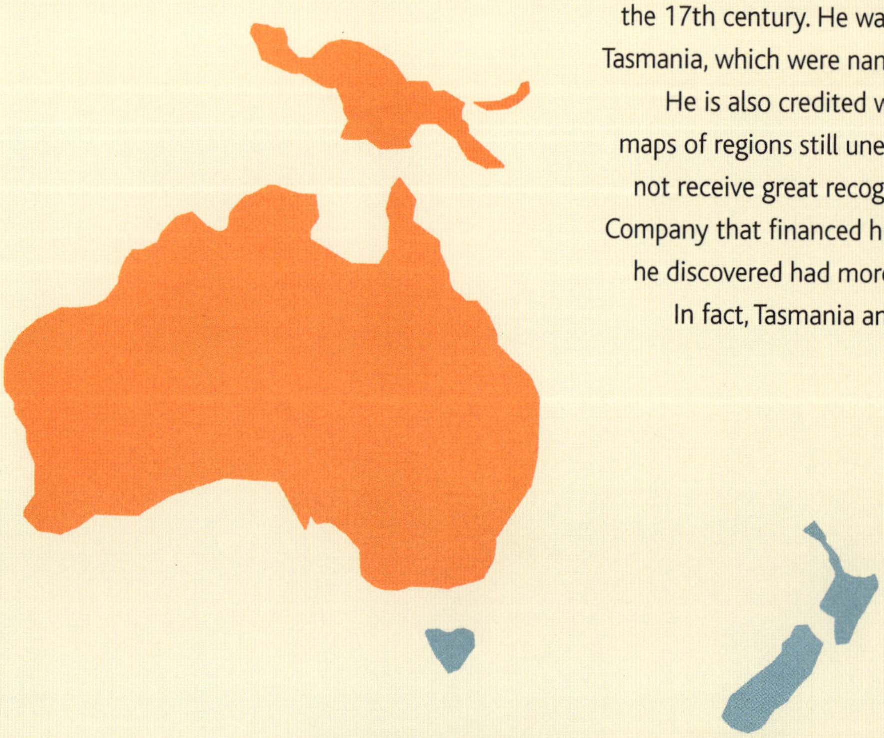

TASMANIAN DEVIL

The Tasmanian devil is a carnivorous marsupial and its name comes from its bad, yet undeserved, reputation of being extremely ferocious. In actual fact, as large as a medium-sized dog, this animal feeds above all on carrion. However, thanks to its very strong bite and proud character, it occasionally hunts prey such as small kangaroos. For centuries it was unjustly persecuted as it was accused of killing domestic animals, which were most probably victims of wild dogs. While it was also originally widespread in Australia, due to indiscriminate hunting, it is now only found in Tasmania and has become a protected species.

NORTH AMERICA

North America is the third largest continent. It stretches from the arctic ice in the north as far as the thin strait of land that separates it from South America.

Its coasts are washed by two oceans, the Atlantic to the east and the Pacific to the west.

This continent contains a huge variety of environments, from deserts and high mountains to plains and forests, which are home to very diverse flora and fauna.

POLAR BEAR

An able swimmer and fierce predator, the polar bear dominates the freezing lands in the north. Its thick white fur provides excellent insulation from the low temperatures and camouflages it among the ice and snow. It lives a solitary life and embarks on long journeys in the search of prey, such as seals.

WALRUS

This is a huge animal that lives in an aquatic environment, typical of cold seas. It has long whiskers and two large canine teeth that it uses to break the ice and also uses as crampons to lift itself out of the water. It loves resting on floating blocks of ice.

MUSKOX

This is a large bovine, covered in thick fur that is so long it touches the ground, protecting it from the cold as it lives in the tundra in Canada and Alaska. Here the summer is cool and short, while the winter is long and harsh.

MOOSE

The moose is the largest representative of the deer family. It has dark grey fur that lightens in winter. It loves humid environments and immersing itself in water. The males have large horns called antlers, which fall off and grow back every year.

BEAVER

Three feet (1 m) in length, the beaver is the largest rodent in North America. It lives in water and has waterproof fur. It is famous for its ability to build dams from tree branches, which block the flow of rivers and create small lakes.

GRIZZLY BEAR

This is a huge brown bear that lives in temperate and cold forests. It is an omnivorous animal and feeds on berries, fruit, and roots, but also meat, including salmon that it skillfully fishes from the rivers and streams. It spends the winter in a deep sleep.

SALMON

This fish embarks on great migrations. It lives in the ocean but returns in great numbers to the river to reproduce. At the source of the river, the female lays its eggs, which are fertilized by the male. The journey is long and dangerous and only a small percentage reach their destination.

BALD EAGLE

Since 1782, this eagle has been the national symbol of the USA. It is a skillful hunter, with fish being its favorite prey. This is why it prefers to live near lakes and waterways. However, its diet also includes snakes, small mammals, and carrion.

SKUNK

This is a nocturnal and omnivorous animal. It defends itself against predators by spraying them with a nauseating liquid produced by glands under its tail.

RACCOON

In some languages the raccoon is named after its unusual habit of washing food in water before eating it. It feeds on small animals and nuts, but often easily finds leftover food from the trash.

PRONGHORN

This is a very fast herbivore that lives in the large grasslands where it feeds on grass and shoots. It has a brown body with a white rear and belly. Its branched horns have an internal bone structure like bovidae, but they fall off every year like deer.

OPOSSUM

This is a small marsupial that lives a solitary life. It spends its days in the trees, often hanging by its long prehensile tail. When it feels threatened, the opossum pretends to be dead to disorient the predator and then escapes at the first chance.

ALLIGATOR

The American alligator lives in the swampy areas, rivers, and lakes of the south-eastern regions of the USA. Its body is armored with bony scales covered in a greenish-brown skin. Alligators effortlessly camouflage themselves in the environment and can easily be mistaken for tree trunks.

PUMA

Also known as a mountain lion, the puma is a large solitary carnivore who prefers a nocturnal and crepuscular life. It lives in various environments, from the mountains to the forests, marking its territory with urine and by leaving scratch marks on tree trunks.

STELLER'S JAY

It has an unusual crest on its head and can mimic sounds. The Steller's jay lives in groups in the forests of North America but, showing no fear of man, it often approaches homes at the edges of forests in search of a meal.

LESSER BLACK-BACKED GULL

This is a medium to large-sized gull that can also be found outside of America. It builds its nest near the coast and lays three eggs there once a year. It looks for food in the sea, but also preys on other sea birds.

PRAIRIE DOG

This is a small rodent that lives in colonies of numerous individuals, inside dens dug into the ground that are linked up by tunnels to form an underground city. There are observation points outside for the sentries who warn their companions by whistling if a predator comes along.

ROAD RUNNER

Related to the cuckoo, though it is able to fly, this small bird prefers running. It catches it prey, generally small animals but also venomous snakes, by chasing them at great speed. Indeed, it can reach up to 18 miles (30 km) per hour. It is the uncatchable bird of Wile E. Coyote in the famous cartoon.

KANGAROO RAT

This is a small rodent from arid regions with long hind legs that enable it to move more easily in the sand by making little bounces. It can survive on very little liquid, getting the water it needs from its diet of seeds and insects.

RATTLESNAKE

This western diamondback rattlesnake injects venom with its bite that is very dangerous even for man. The rattlesnakes can be recognized by the rings of dry skin that remain on their tail after shedding various layers. By shaking its tail, the animal makes its characteristic sound as a warning sign.

CORAL SNAKE

Related to the cobra, this is one of the world's most poisonous snakes. It is easily recognizable due to its bright colors. There are alternating red, yellow, and black bands all along its body. Many innocuous snakes have a similar appearance and take advantage of the fear this snake elicits to scare off potential predators.

SEA LION

This is a very intelligent animal, often used in the circus and marine shows due to its balancing skills. Compared to seals, sea lions have small ear flaps and they can move over land by pushing themselves forwards with their back fins.

MARLIN

This is a fish with a particularly long upper jaw, like a swordfish. It is one of the most highly-esteemed prey in recreational fishing due to its ability and strength. It can also swim very fast and has an aggressive temperament.

GIANT OARFISH

This is a huge abyssal fish that can reach up to 35 feet (11 m) in length. It is a carnivore, but its prey is small in size. Therefore, even though it has given rise to various legends about marine serpents and monsters, this fish is harmless to man.

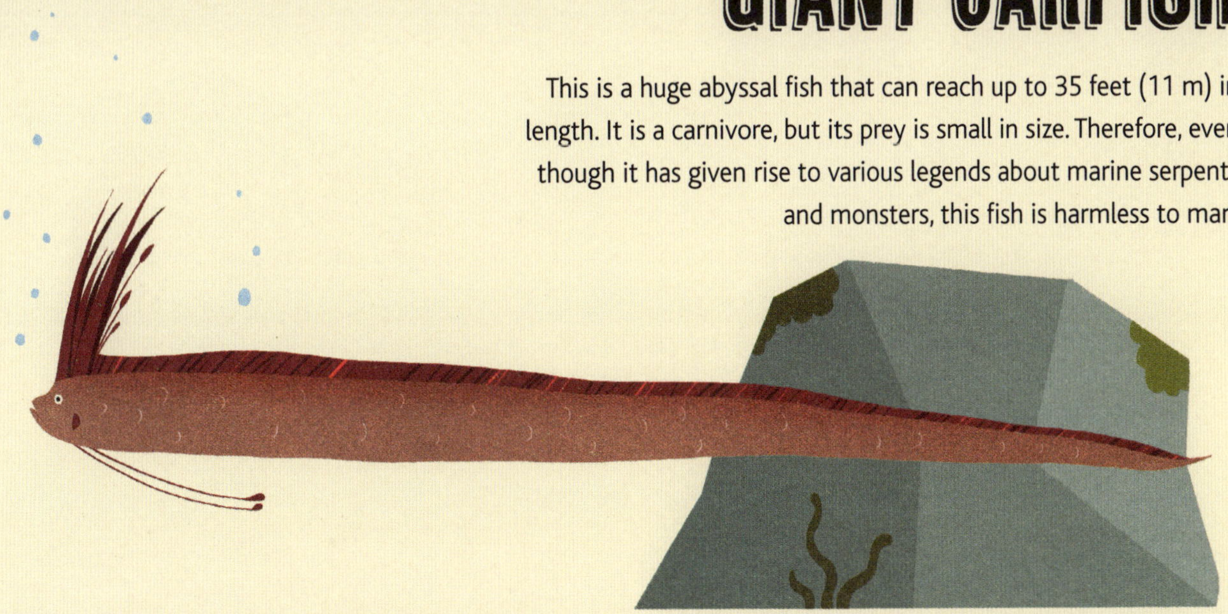

GENERAL ULYSSES SIMPSON GRANT AND THE BISON

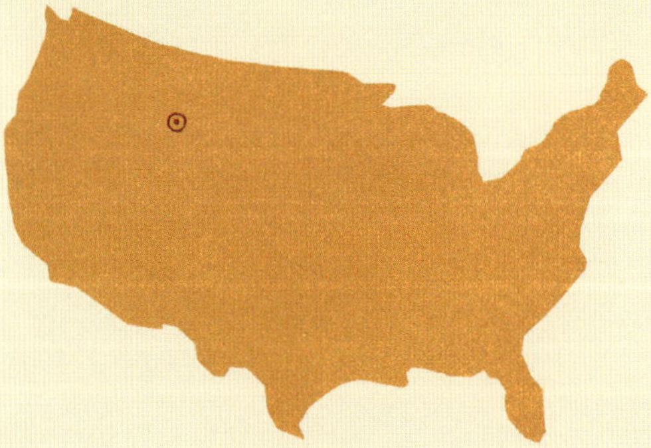

General Grant's name is tied to one of the most important natural parks in the world, Yellowstone Park. In 1872, when he was President of the United States of America, he passed the law that decreed its institution.

The park stretches over the territories of three US states (Wyoming, Idaho, and Montana) and is considered the first ever National Park.

Faced with uncontrolled exploitation of natural resources, the government realized that they needed to preserve a region where nature was still uncontaminated. The park enabled the protection of bison which had been brought to the verge of extinction by ruthless hunting, reduced to less than 100 animals. Today they live in protection and their numbers are increasing.

The bison is a large bovine. It has very long dark fur on its head and shoulders which makes the front of its body very large. Both males and females have long, sharp horns. The bison live in separate herds that reunite only in summer during the mating season. In springtime, the females generally give birth to just one calf.

SOUTH AMERICA

South America is a large continent linked to North America by a thin strip of land called the Isthmus of Panama and is washed by both the Atlantic and Pacific Oceans.

More than 30% of South America is covered in rainforests. Its largest rainforest is the Amazon forest.

It stretches from the tropics almost as far as the South Pole and, due to its size, South America boasts a vast range of climates and habitats. In addition to the forests, there are also high mountains covered in snow, like the Andes, and also deserts and grasslands.

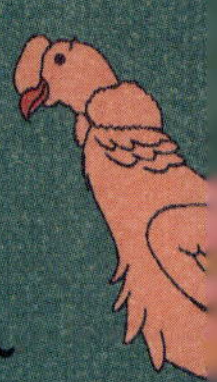

PECCARY

Similar to a pig, the peccary lives in different types of environments, from forests and grasslands to the desert, also easily adapting to the city where it easily finds food, especially among the garbage. The peccary shelters in dens made from caves, cavities in trees, or holes in the ground.

JAGUAR

This is a great American feline, with its characteristic spotted coat which enables it to hide among the trees of the thick rainforests where it lives. It is a skilled hunter that catches its prey by pouncing on it by surprise, preferring to bite the head rather than the neck.

OCELOT

It is similar to a large wild cat. It has spotted fur that allows it to easily hide itself among the forest foliage. It is active at night, while preferring to snooze among the tree branches during the day. Its call to others of its kind is a meow like that of a cat.

HOWLER MONKEY

It has a long prehensile tail that enables it to hang from branches with a tactile zone at the tip. Its name derives from its ability to make extremely loud sounds that can even be heard from several miles away.

TAPIR

Tapirs are large mammals with heavy bodies, large ears, and a short proboscis which the animal uses to bring food to its mouth. The young are mimetic in color at birth and then they get darker with age. Tapirs love water, where they eat, rest, and wash.

SLOTH

The sloth is a lazy mammal that spends its days almost fully immobile, hanging from the highest branches of the trees thanks to its long limbs. It feeds on leaves which it digests very slowly. Its mouth is shaped in such a way that the animal appears to be smiling.

VAMPIRE BAT

This is a small bat that feeds by night on the blood of large mammals, such as cows and horses, while they sleep, without causing them serious harm. They don't suck the blood, but instead they bite the flesh and then lick the blood as it flows out of the small wound. Its saliva contains a substance that prevents the blood from coagulating and thickening.

TOUCAN

Toucans are rainforest birds, well known for their large colorful beaks. They build their nests inside the trees, using holes dug by other animals. They eat fruit, and also small vertebrates and the eggs of other birds. Their small wings prevent them from flying long distances.

QUETZAL

The bright colors of its plumage make this small bird magnificent. The males also have a tuft of feathers that forms a crest over their heads and tailfeathers of up to 3.5 feet (1 m). Due to its beauty, the quetzal was considered a sacred animal by ancient civilizations such as the Aztecs and the Mayas.

AMAZON PARROT

Amazon parrots have been long captured in their natural habitat as they are very popular as domestic animals, not just because of their colors, but also because of their intelligence, funny nature, and very lively character. In addition, they quickly learn to imitate sounds and the human voice.

SPECTACLED CAIMAN

This reptile is related to alligators and crocodiles. Its unusual name derives from the bony ridge in front of its eyes. It is active at night, while during the day it rests immobile in the sun. The nest is a pile of earth 5 feet (1.5 m) long and it can contain up to 65 eggs, which hatch after six weeks.

ANACONDA

Its habitat is the swamps and rivers of the dense Amazon forest. Anacondas are constrictors that kill their prey by wrapping themselves around their bodies and suffocating them among their coils. Their diet includes large rodents, tapirs, deer, fish, turtles, birds, and water reptiles. Occasionally they can even catch jaguars.

PIRANHA

This is a freshwater fish that lives mainly in the rivers of the Amazon forest. It owes its bad reputation to the numerous tiny sharp teeth in its mouth. Indeed, using its strong bite, it can lacerate and tear meat from prey very quickly.

BOA

This is a large constrictor snake that kills its prey by suffocating it and then swallowing it whole, thanks to its particularly flexible jawbones which enable it to open its mouth incredibly wide. Boas are ovoviviparous; 10 to 60 young are born already formed after developing in an egg within the mother's body.

BASILISK

The most unusual characteristic of the basilisk is its ability to walk on water. Indeed, in order to escape predators, it drops down into a puddle and then, running really fast on its hind legs, it avoids sinking thanks to the strips of skin that act as paddles. This is why it is often also called the Jesus Christ lizard.

GREEN IGUANA

Similar to a large lizard, the green iguana lives among the trees of the rainforest. Here it can easily hide itself, thanks to the mimetic color of its skin, which is generally green. However, it can present many different tones that change with age, time of day, gender, and even mood.

COCK-OF-THE-ROCK

The male boasts very gaudy plumage, with coloring that ranges from red to bright orange, while its wings and tail are greyish black. Its head features a small semi-circular crest that is made of feathers, unlike true cocks. It lives near cliffs where the female builds the nest.

HARPY EAGLE

This eagle lives in the rainforests and controls its hunting territory from the tops of the trees. The nest is built by both the male and female at over 320 feet (100 m) high and is almost 6.5 feet (2 m) long. Only one chick is reared in the nest.

HUMMINGBIRD

Hummingbirds are small colorful birds that flap their wings so quickly they buzz like insects. They can fly to the right, to the left, up, down, backwards, and even upside-down. Its long, thin beak is used to gather nectar from the center of flowers.

BLUE-FOOTED BOOBY

This bird can be easily recognized by its light blue feet, which the animal lifts up and down during the mating season in a unique courting dance. Around half of the world's population of boobies lives on the Galapagos Islands.

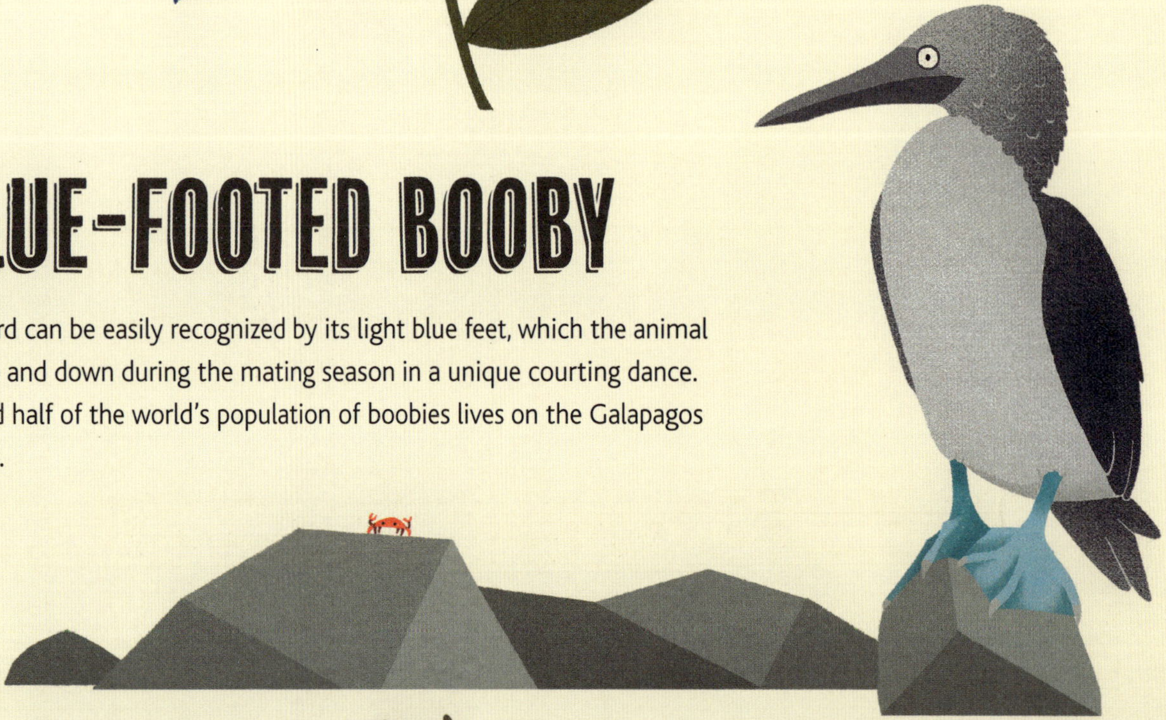

GUANACO

This herbivore is typical of the high mountains. The guanaco lives in the Andes where it can reach high altitudes of up to 13,100 feet (4000 m). Fights between males can be very tough. They chase and bite each other on the neck, pushing violently to try to make their adversary fall to its knees.

ANDEAN CONDOR

This is the largest bird in South America. With a wingspan of 10 feet (3 m) and weighing just 30 pounds (15 kg), it can fly long distances by gliding without needing to flap its wings. It lives in the Andes at heights of over 16,400 feet (5000 m) and generally feeds on carrion.

ARMADILLO

The most obvious characteristic of the armadillo is the armor covering its body. This is formed of various articulated pieces that enable it to roll up in a ball if it feels threatened. Thanks to its long claws, it can dig to look for insects to eat or to build itself a shelter.

MANED WOLF

The maned wolf is a wild dog with long legs which enable it to lightly move among the high grass of the grasslands, which is its typical habitat. Its head is similar to a fox's and it has reddish colored fur. It likes solitary life and is prevalently nocturnal. It feeds on small animals but also loves eating berries.

CHARLES DARWIN AND THE GIANT TORTOISES

Charles Darwin is remembered as the greatest naturalist. As a young man, he had the good fortune to embark on a long journey around the world on a small ship called the Beagle. From 1831 to 1836, he remained far from home, but he had the opportunity to discover environments and animals that he never could have imagined.

Thanks to his careful observations, he hypothesized that all living things change over time, adapting to the natural changes in the environment.

Many years after his return, he published his book "On the Origin of Species" in 1859, where he presented his innovative theory of evolution. This theory was not immediately embraced by his contemporary scientists. They particularly would not accept that man could be related to animals through an ancient common ancestor.

Darwin encountered giant tortoises at the Galapagos Islands. Over 5 feet (1.5 m) in length, they are the largest in the world and are also the longest-living, surviving for up to 150 years!

Like all tortoises, they feed on vegetation. They are peaceful, lazy animals. They spend many hours of the day in the sun to absorb the heat necessary to sustain the metabolism of their large bodies.

ANTARCTICA

Antarctica is a vast continent, one and a half times the size of Europe, which stretches out around the South Pole.

It is almost entirely covered in ice, which can exceed a mile in thickness (1.5 km). Naturally, it is the most inhospitable continent on Earth.

The average temperatures range from -77 °F to -122 °F (-25 °C to -50 °C), reaching record lows of -194 °F (-90 °C).

It is easy to understand why the animals that live in this extreme environment (apart from man) must possess very special adaptations to survive.

EMPEROR PENGUIN

The largest of all penguins, the emperor penguin is over 47 inches (120 cm) tall. The lives of these penguins are regulated by the demands of reproduction, which occurs during the Antarctic winter in extreme conditions at temperatures of -104 °F (-40 °C).

ELEPHANT SEAL

The name "elephant seal" is perfect for this seal. The males grow up to 16 feet (5 m) in length and weigh 3.5 tons, and they also have a type of proboscis.The females, on the other hand, are much smaller: they only reach 10 feet (3 m) in length and 1760 pounds (800 kg) in weight!

ROSS SEAL

This seal gets its name from the Ross Sea. It can reach a maximum of 6.5 feet (2 m) in length and mainly lives in solitude in the extreme environs of the Antarctic ice sheets. For this reason, it is very hard to observe it and study its habits.

WANDERING ALBATROSS

The wandering albatross is a formidable glider and has the largest wingspan of all birds, reaching 11.5 feet (3.5 m). It weighs around 22 pounds (10 kg), but its perfect aerodynamic structure enables it to take advantage of the wind and fly long distances without any effort.

PETREL

The petrel is a sea bird that permanently flies low between waves to catch the fish it feeds on. It only stops during the nesting period, which occurs on the rocky coasts. Only one egg is laid in the nest and it is brooded by both parents.

ANTARCTIC FULMAR

The fulmar is an elegant sea bird that nests in numerous colonies on the Antarctic and sub-Antarctic coasts. Though it is not related to seagulls, the fulmar looks similar to them both in its appearance and habits. It feeds on tiny crustaceans, small fish, and squid.

GREAT SKUA

The great skua is related to seagulls, which it often flocks with, but its intentions are not friendly. In fact, it is not a good fisher. Taking advantage of its large size, it often steals fish from the seagulls, even forcing them to regurgitate it while in flight!

SOUTHERN GIANT PETREL

The southern giant petrel is the largest bird in the Antarctic, with its wingspan reaching over 6.5 feet (2 m). It is great at flying and is a skillful swimmer, able to easily catch the fish it feeds on. However, it often also acts as a scavenger, eating dead animals.

SOUTHERN RIGHT WHALE

The southern right whale has an enormous mouth which it opens wide to seize tons of water containing large quantities of shrimps or "krill", its only nourishment. The baleens it uses to filter the food can reach up to 10 feet (3 m) in length.

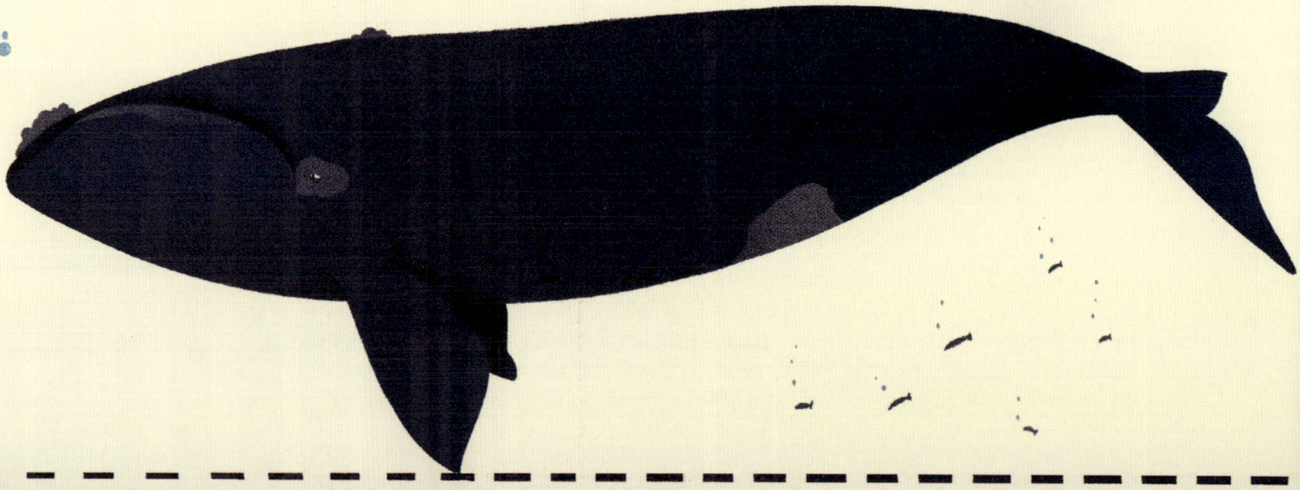

ORCA

The largest predator on the planet, the orca is a cetacean found in all of the oceans. The male can reach up to 30 feet (9 m) in length and when it swims near the surface of the water, you can see its dorsal fin, which it raises more than 10 feet (3 m) over the surface.

ICEFISH

Thanks to dissolved salt, seawater can drop to very low temperatures without freezing. In these cold waters we can find a fish that has anti-freeze in its blood: the icefish! Living in such an inhospitable environment is not easy, but it is one way to have less predators to defend yourself from.

JAMES WEDDELL

Even though the main objective of his voyages was to hunt seals, James Weddell is remembered as a navigator and explorer. Indeed, he was also interested in tracing new routes and discovering unexplored lands.

In 1823, on his brigantine "Jane" in which he had already embarked on various journeys, Weddell headed further and further south until he caught sight of the Antarctic continent. He had reached the area now called Coats Land in the sea that now carries his name, the Weddell Sea. It was the most southern point ever reached at that time.

In a twist of fate, the Weddell seal got its name from one of its most famous hunters. With its length of over 10 feet (3 m) and weighing half a ton, this seal's only predators are the orca and the leopard seal.
The layer of blubber that protects it from the intense cold and its feats in water are unbelievable. Indeed, it can descend to depths of 1970 feet (600 m), holding its breath for up to one hour and twenty minutes. It often swims under the layer of ice and when it needs to return to the surface to breath, if it doesn't find a way out, it can use its front teeth to dig an opening in the sheet of ice above.

FASTEST ANIMALS

Slender, light, and long-legged, the cheetah holds the record for speed in running, reaching 70 miles (110 km) per hour. However, as always, there are other animals that might surprise you in this field.

FRIGATEBIRD

This is a bird with a wingspan of around 6.5 feet (2 m) that can exceed 95 miles per hour (150 km/h). Though it can cover great distances, it can never go into water as its feathers are not waterproof. The male has a bright red pouch on its throat that it puffs up during courting.

SPRINGBOK

This is a rather small and very agile antelope whose habitat is in south-western Africa. It lives in arid environments, but by grazing on succulent plants it does not need to drink. It can reach 55 miles per hour (88 km/h) and, to catch a female's attention, the male can jump 6.5 feet (2 m).

MAKO SHARK

This is a large shark; even the females can reach almost 10 feet (3 m) in length. It can swim far and fast, also thanks to the particularly hydrodynamic shape of its head. With sprints of 43 miles per hour (68 km/h), it can catch up with really fast fish, such as tuna.

SLOWEST ANIMALS

Every living creature has developed its own survival strategy and, as well as animals that use lightning-fast sprints for defense or attack, others prefer not to bring attention to themselves, moving slowly or remaining anchored in their shelter.

MANATEE

These are also called sea cows because they feed on the vegetation in marine grasslands. Lacking in incisors or canine teeth, the manatee only has molars and premolars. Subject to heavy use, these are constantly replaced. The manatee can weigh up to 1100 pounds (500 kg) and swims very slowly, reaching a maximum of 3-5 miles per hour (5-8 km/h).

LORIS

Measuring around 10 inches (25 cm) in length, this little primate lives in the rainforests of Sri Lanka and spends its life in the trees. A nocturnal animal, it has huge eyes and spends the entire day curled up sleeping. It moves particularly slowly, even stopping between each step. However, when it needs to catch prey, it can reach 1.3 miles per hour (2 km/h).

SEAHORSE

Though it assumes a more hydrodynamic position while swimming, the seahorse is structured to stay upright and anchor itself in vegetation with its prehensile tail. Its average speed is just 0.05 miles per hour (0.09 km/h)! The male has a pouch where the female lays the eggs and the fry develop.

LARGEST ANIMALS

The largest animal of them all is the blue whale, which can exceed 110 feet (33 m) in length and 180 tons in weight. However, each group of animals has its own "giant" whose size might surprise you.

GIANT SALAMANDER

Typically aquatic and nocturnal, it can live for over 50 years and uses touch more than sight to catch its prey. The giant salamander lives in Japan and China, but it is the Chinese species that holds the record for size, as it can reach 70 inches (180 cm) in length and 130 pounds (59 kg) in weight.

BELUGA

It is the female of this species that holds the record, measuring 30 feet (9 m) in length and 3300 pounds (1500 kg) in weight. This giant lives in the freshwaters between Europe and Asia, feeding on aquatic invertebrates. Its eggs, more that 7 million per female, are one of the most coveted types of caviar.

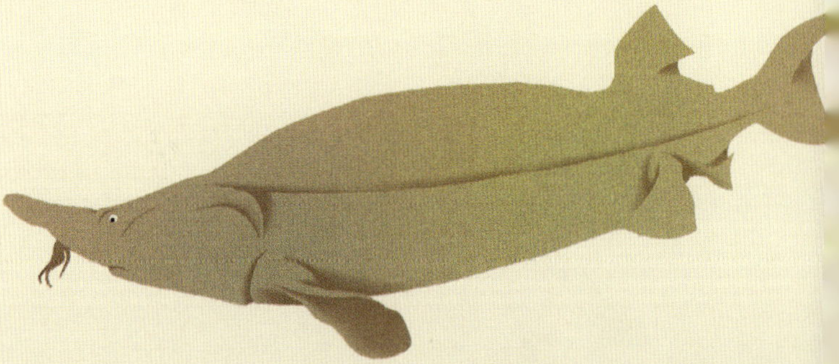

CAPYBARA

Small ears and a short tail are typical of this giant rat that grows up to 53 inches (135 cm) in length and 130 pounds (60 kg) in weight. It lives peacefully along the waterways of South America, feeding on aquatic plants, corn, and sugarcane.

SMALLEST ANIMALS

Scientists declared in 2012 that the smallest vertebrate in the world is a frog from Papua New Guinea. With a length of 0.3 inches (0.77 cm), it beat the record of a small Asian fish by just 0.007 inches (0.02 cm). Extremely agile, it can jump up to 30 times the length of its body.

BARBADOS THREADSNAKE

Its name tells you just how thin this snake is, reaching just 4 inches (10 cm) in length. Grayish in color, it lives in the Caribbean and feeds on termites and their larva. The female lays just one egg, from which a baby snake about half the size of an adult emerges.

PYGMY MARMOSET

It lives in the Amazon forest and measures about 12 inches (30 cm) in length, half of which is its tail. A light animal, weighing approximately 4.5 ounces (130 g), it lives in trees and can reach the ends of branches to feed on fruit and insects without any competitors. It is always born with a twin and is also reared by the father.

BROOKESIA

This tiny chameleon lives in Madagascar and, unlike others of its species, it does not have a prehensile tail and has a limited ability to change its colors. It reaches 1.10 inches (2.9 cm) in length – including the tail!

EXTINCT ANIMALS

Over the Earth's history, many species of animals have become extinct due to natural causes. Even though extinction may be the destiny of most living creatures, man has unfortunately contributed to speeding up the disappearance of some of them, especially through hunting, the destruction of their natural habitats, and pollution.

QUAGGA

The quagga was a type of zebra once widespread in the plains of South Africa. It was hunted for its very unusual coat, which had considerable stripes like zebras, but only in the front part of its body. The last of its species, a female, died in an Amsterdam zoo in 1883.

DODO

This large, peaceful flightless bird lived on the island of Mauritius. Rats, dogs, and pigs arrived on the island with ships from Europe and proceeded to devour the eggs and chicks in their nests. Together with the uncontrolled hunting of man, this led to the extinction of the dodo in 1681, just 100 years after it had been discovered.

THYLACINE

Also called the "Tasmanian tiger", it looked like a dog with a striped coat. The thylacine lived on the large islands of Oceania and it was a carnivorous marsupial. Blaming it for repeated ferocious attacks on livestock, man hunted it to extinction. The last of its kind died in 1936 in a zoo where it had been confined.

AUROCH

This was a large bovine with big forward-curving horns that populated the steppes of Europe and central Asia. It is considered an ancestor of modern cattle. Due to its aggressive character, in Ancient Rome the auroch was often used in arena fights. It disappeared forever in 1627.

MOA

The moa was a gigantic bird, more than 11.5 feet in height (3.5 m), and was similar to an ostrich. A much-coveted prey for hunters for its meat and beautiful feathers, it became extinct in the mid-1400s, just 200 years after the first men arrived in the moa's native New Zealand from the Polynesian islands.

The Steller's sea cow was a huge marine mammal who lived in the freezing waters of the Pacific Ocean. With a peaceful temperament and slow swimming style, these animals were easily hunted by sailors who obtained abundant meat and blubber from them. They were declared extinct in 1768, just 27 years after they had been first discovered by Europeans.

STELLER'S SEA COW

GIULIA LOMBARDO

Giulia is an illustrator who lives and works in Florence (Italy). After graduating from high school specializing in humanities, she decided to completely change her direction of studies. Following her passion, she enrolled in the Nemo Academy of Digital Arts in Florence, graduating with honors in 2013 as an Entertainment Designer. Since then, she has been working as a freelance illustrator in the children's book market, and as a graphic designer and web designer. In recent years, she has illustrated various titles for White Star Kids.

ASSOCIAZIONE DIDATTICA MUSEALE (DIDACTIC MUSEUM ASSOCIATION)

Founded in 1994, Associazione Didattica Museale (ADM) has been working in the education sector for over twenty years. It manages the educational services of top museums such as the Natural History Museums of Milan, Genoa, Novara, and Trieste, as well as organising the didactics of public and private sanctuaries and natural parks. The text of this book was written by Cristina Banfi, Rita Mabel Schiavo and Cristina Peraboni, founding members of the Associazione Didattica Museale – ADM (1994) and ADMaiora srl (2015).

Cristina Banfi A graduate in Natural Sciences from Università degli Studi, Milan, Cristina has taught at various schools. For over twenty years, she has been working in scientific communication and teaching through play. She also has varied editorial experience in both scholastic and educational fields, especially for the children and young adult sector.

Rita Mabel Schiavo A graduate in Biological Sciences specialized in Natural Sciences from Università degli Studi, Milan, Rita continued to pursue her studies, focusing above all on herpetology and eco-ethology.

Cristina Peraboni A veterinarian who has been an enthusiast of natural sciences her entire life, Cristina has always been involved in scientific popularization and edutainment, in addition to giving refresher courses for teachers and training courses for museum educators. She also works with various publishing houses, writing for both children and adults.

WS Kids
WHITE STAR KIDS

White Star Kids® is a registered trademark property of White Star s.r.l.

Piazzale Luigi Cadorna, 6
20123 Milan, Italy
www.whitestar.it

Translation: Langue&Parole, Milan

ISBN 978-88-544-1526-3
1 2 3 4 5 6 23 22 21 20 19

Printed in China